# FROG COUNTS TO TEN

## By John Liebler

THE MILLBROOK PRESS
BROOKFIELD, CONNECTICUT

# For Fawcett

Library of Congress Cataloging-in-Publication Data
Liebler, John.
Frog counts to ten / by John Liebler.
p.   cm.
Summary: Unable to play hide-and-seek because he cannot
count, Frog goes for a ride on his bicycle and makes a discovery.
ISBN 1-56294-436-3 (lib.)          ISBN 1-56294-739-7 (TR.)
ISBN 1-56294-698-6 (pbk. ed.)
[1. Frogs—Fiction.   2. Bicycles and bicycling—Fiction.
3. Counting.]   I. Title.   II. Title: Frog counts to 10.
PZ7.L61645Fr   1994
[E]—dc20   93-40116   CIP   AC

Published by The Millbrook Press
2 Old New Milford Road
Brookfield, Connecticut 06804

Frog could not play hide-and-seek with the other animals because he could not count to ten.

He was one lonely frog.

So, he went for a ride on his two-wheeled bicycle.

He was coasting along at three miles per hour,

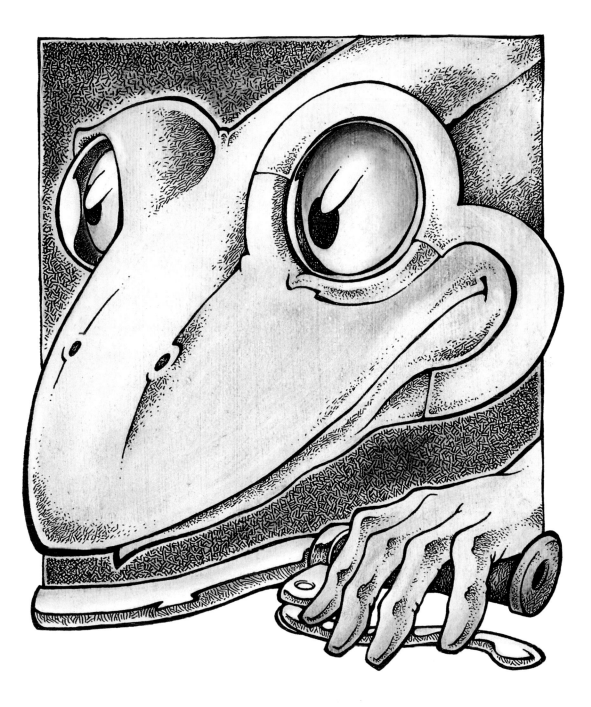

when he was distracted
by four flies . . .

. . . and accidentally rode off a five-foot drop.

He bounced six times on
the way down and landed
on his head.

He saw seven stars . . .

. . . and eight doctors.

The doctors gave him nine bandages . . .

. . . and a bill for ten dollars!

That night, Frog couldn't sleep, so he thought about the day he'd had. He thought about:

—how he'd been *one* lonely frog

—on a *two*-wheeled bicycle

—coasting at *three* miles per hour . . .

And then he realized . . .

# HE COULD COUNT TO TEN!

The next day, Frog told the other animals about his adventure and what he had learned. Then he announced: "Now I can play hide-and-seek because I can count to ten!"

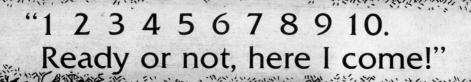

# About
# the Author

John Liebler is a freelance illustrator who lives and works in Hamden, Connecticut. He believes everyone should be able to count.

"I learned to count at an early age," says John, "and I hope to someday be able to count to a million—in dollars."

When he's not working, John, like Frog, enjoys riding his bicycle. Unlike Frog, however, he always wears a helmet and rarely eats flies.